Tales FROM THE Woodpecker Tree

Lesley Rawlinson

by
LESLEY RAWLINSON

Illustrated _by_ Carole Chevalier

ISBN 978-1975602109

Contents

Dedication

For my mother and father,
who always encouraged me to follow
my dreams and climb my very own
Woodpecker Tree.

A Duck for Dinner

Mrs Duck was dozing in the shade of the trees, enjoying the peace of a summer's afternoon. Little did she know but Jo-jo, the big black and white cat, was watching, and thinking how nice it would be to have duck for dinner.

Now Jo-jo wasn't really a hunter. In fact, he was very happy to have his dinner put on his plate every night, without having to go to the trouble of hunting for it. But the thought of Mrs Duck for dinner was very tempting, and it didn't look as if it would be hard work to catch her. Jo-jo didn't like hard work.

Mrs Duck was just dreaming of having a nice paddle in the nearby pond, when a large furry paw tapped her on the head. She opened her eyes and was slightly worried to see a large black and white shape blocking out the sun.

"Do you mind?" she quacked, indignantly. "You're disturbing me!"

Jo-jo frowned. He rather hoped that Mrs Duck would be so frightened, that she'd hop obligingly into his waiting jaws, but that obviously wasn't going to happen.

So, there was only one thing to do...

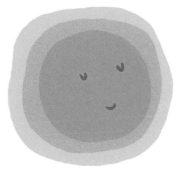

Jo-jo pounced. Before Mrs Duck could quack for help, or flap her wings, he had gathered a mouthful of her feathers and had started to drag her across the grass.

Now, Mrs Duck did not like this one bit. It was very uncomfortable being hauled along by your tail feathers, especially on a hot day. But what was a duck to do? Along the road they went, up the garden path and round to the back door of Jo-jo's house.

"Do you know," said Mr Sharp, from the house next door, "but I've just seen next door's cat with a duck in its mouth?"

"Well! Whatever next?" tutted Mrs Sharp.

What happened next was the appearance of the cat flap. Mrs Duck had never seen one before and here she was having her face pushed into this strange flappy thing.

"Go on!" instructed Jo-jo, crossly. "I want my dinner!"

"Well, really!" thought Mrs Duck. "Does he expect me to cook his dinner? It's not what ducks do!"

With one big push, Jo-jo propelled Mrs Duck through the cat flap, and before you could say "roast duck" they were in the kitchen. Mrs Duck sat and studied her reflection in the oven door. Jo-jo sat by the living room door and waited.

"MEOOOW!"

"Was that the cat?" asked Dad, peering over the top
of the newspaper.

"MEOOOOOW!"

"I think so dear," replied Mum. "I expect he wants his dinner. I'll go
and feed him…"

"DAD! THERE'S A DUCK IN THE KITCHEN!"

"Do you know?" remarked Dad, "I could have sworn Mum just said
there was a duck in the kitchen."

"SHE DID!" shouted Mum. "A REAL, LIVE DUCK!"

"Well, that's nice to know," thought Mrs Duck.
"I was getting worried."

"Meooow?" queried Jo-jo, hopefully. Didn't anyone
understand why he'd parked a nice juicy duck in front
of the oven door?

Mum and Dad looked thoughtfully at Mrs Duck.

"Well," began Mum, "there's only one thing for it.
Pass me the oven gloves!"

"YES!" thought Jo-jo.

"NO!" panicked Mrs Duck.

Mum slipped her hands into the oven gloves, bent down to Mrs Duck and very gently picked her up.

"Come on," she said. "Let's get you...back to the pond!"

"NO!" wailed Jo-jo.

"YES!" sighed a relieved Mrs Duck.

So, much to the surprise of the neighbours, Mum marched up the road, carefully carrying Mrs Duck in her oven gloves. When they reached the pond, she crouched down and placed her in the water. With a satisfied quack and a wiggle of her tail Mrs Duck paddled off to tell Mr Duck about her adventure.

Jo-jo? Well he didn't have duck for dinner.
He had fish.
But that's another story.

Koji's Smile

Koji was the little boy who never smiled. He lived in the big house at the foot of the mountain, with his happy, loving family, but he never smiled.

Every day he would sit in his beautiful playroom, surrounded by all his lovely toys. Every day his brothers and sisters tried to play games with him. But still, Koji never smiled.

His mother and father were very worried so they called the village wise-woman and begged her to help. She listened and looked deep into Koji's sad eyes, then nodded.

"Koji, you must go to the Great Temple, at the top of the mountain. There you will find the Box of Happiness. Ask the Guardian of the Box to let you look inside. That is where you will find your smile." So, the very next morning, Koji put on his sandals and set off up the twisty mountain path.

He hadn't gone far, when he came to a grassy clearing by the river. Koji stopped to drink and, as he sat on a rock, out of the forest gambolled some bear cubs. He watched them roll in the grass and splash in the river, trying to catch the fish which darted among the rocks.

"Are you happy?" asked Koji.

"Of course," cried the bear cubs. "We can play in the grass and try to catch the cherry blossom which floats down from the trees! Will you play too?"

"I have to climb to the Great Temple, to find the Box of Happiness," said Koji.

"Come back soon then!" called the bear cubs, and they gave him a sprig of cherry blossom as a gift.

Koji bowed and carried on up the path, sniffing the sweet perfume of the blossom as he walked.

After a while, he came to a very tall tree at the edge of the forest and perched at the very top was a beautiful white stork.

"Are you happy?" called Koji.

"Of course!" exclaimed the stork. "I fly on the wind and feel it ruffle my feathers. I watch the sun rise and set over the mountains. Will you fly with me Koji?"

"I have to climb to the Great Temple and find the Box of Happiness," replied Koji.

"Good luck!" said the stork, plucking a glistening white feather from his wing and sending it floating down for Koji to catch.

Koji bowed and carried on up the mountain path.

Sometime later he came to a deep, still pool, hidden in a rocky cleft beside the path. Water lilies floated on the dark surface, their pink flowers open to welcome the rays of the sun as it dipped towards the horizon.

On one of these lily pads sat a frog, basking in the afternoon sun. Koji knelt by the pool, scooping its clear icy water into his hands to drink and cool his face.

"Are you happy?" whispered Koji, to the frog.

"Of course!" croaked the frog. "I look at the reflection of the clouds in the water, spotting the patterns they make as they drift across the sky. I swim in the pool and talk to the fishes.
Will you swim with me?"

Koji peered into the pool and spied a shiny pebble among the feathery weeds below the surface. He reached into the icy water and picked it up.

"I have to climb to the Great Temple and find the Box of Happiness," explained Koji, "but may I take this lovely smooth pebble with me?"

"Why, yes!" replied the frog. "Travel safely, little one!"
And with a hop and a plop he had gone!

Koji scrambled to his feet and set off on the last part of his journey. The path took him higher, past rocks where lizards lay in the sun, then darted into cracks as he came by. He saw bright blue flowers hiding in rocky corners, on sparkling beds of snow. An eagle circled high above, gradually drifting down to settle on the golden roof of the Great Temple, where it watched the little boy toiling up the slope towards him.

At last Koji was there. The temple glowed orange in the sunlight and carved golden dragons guarded the high wooden doors. Nervously, Koji approached the doorway and stepped inside. A simple stone table stood on the rocky floor. On the table, lit by the rays of the sun, was a small wooden box. No statues, no ornaments, no fine decorations, just a table and a little box.

As he looked, Koji heard a tapping noise from a dark corner. Turning, he saw a tiny old man, wearing shabby robes. He sat cross-legged on the floor, carving a piece of wood. His long silver hair and beard framed a smiling face which was as brown and wrinkled as a walnut.

"Welcome, Koji," smiled the Guardian of the Box. "Why have you come to see me?"

"I need to find my smile please," said Koji, bowing low.

"Well," replied the old man, "you may open the box!"

Hardly daring to breathe, Koji ran his fingers over the smooth, light wood, until he found two tiny handles. With one gentle pull, the doors swung open.

Koji stared. Tiny shelves opened out on each side, and two beautifully carved drawers, so small that even his tiny fingers fumbled to open them. The first drawer was empty. But in the second was...a tiny mirror!

 Koji turned a puzzled face to the old man. "Where is my smile?" he asked.

"Empty your pockets, Koji!" was the reply.

Frowning, Koji carefully reached into his pockets and placed a sprig of cherry blossom, a feather and a shiny pebble on the table.

As he did, he remembered bear cubs tumbling and laughing by a stream, the stork gliding on the wind above fields and villages, the fish leaping and the frog swimming in the deep mountain pool.

"Now!" said the Guardian of the Box, "look in your mirror."

Koji did as he was told and gasped. Looking back was, of course, his own face. His smiling, happy, (and slightly grubby) face!

"You see! There are lots of beautiful things around us to make us smile," explained the old man. "You must take your treasures home with you now, inside your very own Box of Happiness."

Laughing, Koji put his gifts into the drawers and on the shelves, before carefully closing the doors. He bowed his thanks to the Guardian of the Box then, clutching his box tightly, he ran outside and, singing and dancing, made his way back down the path.

The old man stood smiling, watching the little figure until he was out of sight.

Then slowly, he turned and went inside the temple. In the corner, hidden in the shadows, was an old cupboard. Opening it, he reached inside and took out a small wooden box and, very carefully, placed it on the table.

We all need a magic Box of Happiness, and someone else would be sure to come along soon...

Rock Star Tiger!

It's a hard life being a famous rock star. Especially if you are a toy tiger. But Chester, the favourite cuddly toy in Alice's toy box, was determined to be the coolest cat in town.

Today, Chester was particularly cross. Alice and Mum had taken him to the shops and that meant a buggy ride.

He had been sucked, chewed and licked. He had been bounced, waved about and dropped. And now he was face down in the remains of Alice's sticky bun. So, with coloured, sugary sprinkles stuck to his face, he made his Big Decision.

"I am going to run away!" he growled. "I wasn't meant to be a sticky-bun-faced tiger. I am a tiger with attitude!"

The buggy bounced up a step into a shop where music boomed and thumped.

With a wiggle and a twitch, Chester slipped and slid off Alice's knee and was soon lost among feet and shopping bags. Sitting in a corner, he listened and watched. He decided he liked the music. It made his paws tap and he began to hum.

"I'm a Cool Cat!" thought Chester. "I'm the coolest of all the cats.
I'm going to be... A ROCK STAR!"

So, Chester the rock star, danced.
He rocked and rolled.
He jiggled and jived.
He twirled and twizzled.
He boogied and...bounced, down the stairs and out of the shop.

"Oh look! Someone's lost their teddy!" growled a voice.

"Excuse me, I am not a teddy!" exclaimed Chester. "I'm a ... Aah!
Oof! Gerroff!"

"Well, what are you then?" demanded the large shaggy dog that
was poking a very wet nose into his ear. "And why have you got
sparkly bits on your face?"

"I'm a rock star," announced Chester. "STOP LICKING MY FACE!"

"You're a funny looking rock star. More like a chewed slipper," said
the dog rudely. "Oops! Watch out for that seagull!"

"What seagull? Aargh!" Before Chester could say any more, he
was whisked and whirled high up into the air.
"PUT ME DOWN!" he howled. "I'm a r-r-rock s-s-star!"
"A rock star?" squawked the greedy gull. "I thought you were a
large fish and chip sandwich."

Chester's eyes were tight shut and his tummy
wobbled and wibbled.
"Urrgh!" he groaned.

"Oh well," sighed the gull. "I don't fancy a furry fish
and chip sandwich with sparkly sprinkles anyway.
"Bye!" The next minute Chester was falling. Down,
down, down... SPLASH! Into the river!

Water filled his eyes, ears and nose.
He gurgled and gulped.
He spluttered and splashed.

"HELP!" roared Chester. "I CAN'T SWIM!"

"Really?" hissed a voice. "Well there's no need to make
such a racket."
A graceful swan glided over and daintily pushed a very soggy
Chester with her beak.

"Climb on my back," she offered, "but kindly,
try not to make a mess."

Gratefully, Chester hauled himself up into the soft, warm feathers.
Shivering and shaking, snuffling and sniffling, he sat there in a
miserable heap.

"What are you?" asked the swan, curiously. "You look like a furry
clown fish. And what are those coloured spots on your nose?"

"I'm not any kind of fish," muttered Chester, "or a sandwich. Or a chewed slipper. Or…sniff… a rock star. I'm a tiger."

"Funny sort of a tiger," murmured the swan. "Now, snuggle down in my feathers. I don't want the neighbours to see me in such disreputable company."

Chester was too tired to argue. He crawled into the warmth of the swan's feathers and fell fast asleep.

He didn't feel the gentle rocking as she paddled down the river. He didn't feel the rush of the wind as she flew over the rooftops and out of the city. He didn't feel the dip and dive as she landed. Then she gave herself an ENORMOUS shake!
"Waah! What?" gabbled Chester.

"Get down!" ordered the swan.

"Where am I?" came the dizzy reply from among the feathers.

"At the zoo."
"THE ZOO?"

Chester emerged blinking, lost his balance and fell to the ground in a tangle of fur and feathers.

"Safely home," smiled the swan, straightening her ruffled feathers.
"But…" began Chester.

"Good-bye!" she called, as she flew away. "It looks like your dad is pleased to see you."

"Dad?"
Chester turned.
Chester gulped.
Chester's legs began to wobble.

A magnificent tiger began to pad slowly towards him. He could see its sharp pointy teeth and hear its deep rumbling growl. Chester had a nasty feeling that THIS was a tiger with attitude. A very cool cat indeed.

He ran as fast as his furry legs could carry him.
Puffing and panting. (Watch out he's coming!)
Gasping and grunting. (Almost there!)
Coughing and choking, (Two more steps!)
He fell through the railings and landed at someone's feet.

"CHESTER!" squealed Alice's voice. "Where have you been? We've looked everywhere!"

"Chester?" cried Mum, picking him up. "Ugh…"

Later that night, bathed and brushed, Chester snuggled up to Alice. He didn't want to be a rock star. He didn't want to be a cool cat. He was happy to be Alice's cuddly tiger. With just a few coloured sprinkles on his nose.

Wilberforce Learns a Lesson

Colin's garden was a magical place. On one side was the old farmhouse, with climbing plants and old rose bushes scrambling up its walls. On every other side, hills, fields and woodland stretched as far as you could see, and the sheep and cows grazed, munched and chomped contentedly in the sunshine.

But, inside the garden, amongst the tangle of colourful bushes and flowers, the birds had their home.

Darting to and from the nut feeder on the old beech tree, were the finches, sparrows and any number of blue tits and great tits. Pecking fussily among the bushes, clucking musically to themselves, were the hens, Harriet and Martha, while the cockerel, Arthur, strutted bossily around them.

Then there were Cuthbert and Clarence. Not the sort of birds you would normally expect to see in an ordinary country garden, but Colin's garden was different. Look over the hedge and you will see on top of the bird table, mooching amongst the fruit bushes, or even balanced on the branches of the tree, two very pompous but glorious peacocks. Don't ask me how they got there – but this is their home. (Colin might tell you, if you ask him nicely.)

It was a hot summer's day. Bees buzzed lazily among the flowers, with butterflies weaving and dancing around them. Swallows and house martins looped and chirruped over the farmhouse, diving and swooping after the flies.

Clarence rested on the top of the bird table, with one beady eye fixed on the bird feeder, which swung and twirled, as two young chaffinches, Chideock and Chesil, pecked hungrily at the nuts. Clarence contemplated trying to have a peck himself, but decided it could lead to the demolition of the feeder, and possibly the tree too. So, with a sigh, he resumed the job of cleaning and preening his magnificent feathers.

"Gerroff!! Mine! Mine!"

The sudden squawk and flurry of feathers nearly made Clarence fall off his perch. Cuthbert erupted from his snoozing place under a bush and the sparrows flew around in a frenzy of twittering. Chideock and Chesil were fluttering about on the grass, and staring in amazement at a striking black and white bird, with a red cap, very sharp beak and an angry look in his eye. Wilberforce, the baby woodpecker, had arrived.

All that day the birds tried to get on with their usual activities. But, every time their beaks found an interesting berry, seed or nut, Wilberforce's bright eyes would spot them and:

"Gerroff!! Mine! Mine!"

At one point, Cuthbert strutted over to have a stern word with the naughty little bird, but Wilberforce had spotted one of his gorgeous blue feathers, looking just a little bit ruffled. As Cuthbert opened his beak to speak, he felt a sharp twinge and – ouch!! Wilberforce was dancing down the garden with the feather sprouting from his beak.

"Why, you little…!" spluttered Cuthbert. He glared about him. "Where is your mother?"

Poor Mrs. Woodpecker. That evening, when the baby birds had been shooed off to roost, she sat in the branches of the old beech tree, while the rest of the birds clustered around, all talking at once.

"Can't you do something with him?" demanded Mr. Chaffinch. "My Chesil and Chideock are too frightened to come into the garden now!"

"I can't do a thing with him!" wailed Mrs. Woodpecker. "He just won't listen to me at all."

"We could 'ave a word with 'im," offered a distinctly grubby pigeon, sitting on the nearby roof. A crowd of his friends cooed and nodded beside him, having flown over from the farmyard to watch the fun.

"We don't need advice from your sort, thank you!" snapped Mrs. Blackbird.

"Please yourselves," sniffed the pigeons, and they flew off, cooing rudely at the other birds.

"Ooh! They are just the sort I'm afraid Wilberforce will get involved with!" cried his mother anxiously, hopping from one leg to another. "What shall we do?"

It was Mrs. Wagtail who came up with the answer. Sitting quietly on the edge of the group, she suddenly began bobbing up and down with excitement.

"I know! I know!" she cried. "But we will need some help…" And she nodded up to the sky where, far above, two dark shapes glided and circled silently in the evening light.

When Wilberforce woke the next morning, he immediately fluffed up his feathers, and headed down the hill and over the hedge into Colin's garden. The bird feeder was hanging in its usual place, swaying in the breeze, and Wilberforce set to, nibbling and pecking at the nuts. After a few minutes, he looked around, eager to see what everyone else was up to. But there was no one to be seen. The leaves rustled on the tree, but no birds hopped along the branches. Looking around, Wilberforce suddenly realised that he was completely alone. No birds circled overhead, no twittering came from the bushes. Everywhere was completely, totally silent.

Suddenly feeling very lonely and frightened, Wilberforce was about to fly back to hide in his nest when he spotted something moving among the fruit bushes. It was Clarence! With a squawk, Wilberforce flew down to join the peacock who was delicately pecking at some blackberries. Clarence glanced at the little woodpecker and seemed surprised to see him.

"What are you doing here?" he asked. "Everyone else has gone to the wood."

"The wood?" Wilberforce was puzzled. His mother had told him to keep away from there, as it was dangerous for baby birds to explore on their own.

"Ooh, yes!" exclaimed Clarence. "There are some lovely places to feed there. You'll be missing all the fun!"

That was enough for Wilberforce. The thought of other birds getting something, and not him, was too much to bear. Pausing only to grab a blackberry from Clarence's beak, he swooped up and over the hedge, and across the hillside towards the wood. He didn't see the dozens of pairs of eyes watching from inside the bushes and hedgerows. The plan was working!

Although the sun was shining brightly, inside the wood it was dark and still. Wilberforce had dived in among the tangle of branches without thinking, and now he perched nervously on a wobbly twig listening for familiar twitterings and hoping to see a bird he knew.

The leaves rustled over his head, and Wilberforce looked up quickly to see who, or what, was there. Nothing.

A magpie cackled loudly somewhere, and Wilberforce jumped in the air with a squeak of fright. But nothing came near.

"Mummy!!" howled Wilberforce, and he fluttered his wings as he tried to pluck up courage to fly through the trees and find a way out of the wood.

But just at that moment, a shadow passed over his head. Wilberforce felt something brush against him and then a beak grab him by the neck. Before he could wriggle away, he felt himself flying up through the trees. There was a dizzying look-out over the tops of the trees, and then he was dropped with a thump into a nest.

For a moment, Wilberforce cowered down among the twigs then slowly lifted his head. Glaring down at him, were two large brown birds, with fierce eyes, very sharp beaks, and vicious looking talons. Even Wilberforce knew who these kings of the sky were. Buzzards!!

"So, this is the little troublemaker!" snapped Benjamin Buzzard. "We've heard a lot about you."

"Hmm, yes," nodded his friend Beatrice. "I like the look of those feathers. I could use them to line the nest!"

"Well, why not?" grinned Benjamin. "No one will come looking for him. They will be glad to get rid of someone so mean and unkind."
"Oh, but I didn't mean to be unkind!" cried Wilberforce.
"Oh, I want my mummy!!"

Just at that moment, there was a loud flapping of wings, a cry of, "Oh crikey!" and the whole tree seemed to shake. The nest wobbled dangerously and Wilberforce closed his eyes.

"Oh, I hate heights!" spluttered a familiar voice.

Wilberforce opened his eyes, and let out a squeak of delight.
"Cuthbert!" he cried.

The peacock wobbled along the branch, and poked his beak at the two buzzards.

"Now, I don't want to hang around up here any longer than I need to," began Cuthbert.

"Good!" muttered Beatrice, who was getting worried about the safety of the branch. Another minute and they would all be on the ground.

"If this young creature agrees to behave himself, will you let him go?" asked Cuthbert.

"Oh, I will, I will!" chirped Wilberforce loudly, before anyone else could speak.

The branch creaked and trembled alarmingly, as Cuthbert tried to balance on one leg, and scratch his head.

"Watch what you're doing!" snapped Benjamin. "All right, you can take him, but…" and he poked his beak dangerously close to the terrified young woodpecker, "any more greedy behaviour and we will be watching!"

Wilberforce hopped out of the nest as fast as he could and tottered along the branch to Cuthbert. Over the top of his head, the peacock nodded to the buzzards, and winked.

"Just a minute!" cried Beatrice, as Cuthbert made a few cautious flaps of his wings to remind them how to fly.

"Could you leave me one of your lovely feathers? It would add such a nice touch to my nest!"

"If I lose any more I'll be bald," grumbled Cuthbert, but he waggled his huge tail at the buzzards, and Beatrice deftly tweaked one feather out.

Then, with a flurry of wings, and an alarming wobble, Cuthbert fell off the branch. Wilberforce squeaked with fright, but he flapped his own little wings and leapt into the air. Cuthbert plunged down through the branches, and managed to land in the field beside the wood, narrowly missing several sheep on the way. Wilberforce flew down and landed too, as his friend picked leaves and twigs out of his beautiful feathers.

"Thank you, Cuthbert," he whispered. "I promise I will be good now, and kind to the other birds."

"Hmm!" grunted Cuthbert. "Well, I hope so. Come on, let's get back to the garden. The others are waiting."

Back in Colin's garden, the feeder swung in the breeze, as several young sparrows nibbled at the nuts. Goldfinches pecked at seed heads, pied wagtails and blackbirds searched the grass for worms. Mrs. Woodpecker sat on a branch in the old beech tree, watching proudly as her young son flew down to join the sparrows, sharing the nuts with them and carefully tossing one or two down to the chaffinches on the ground. Clarence was on the bird table, listening to his friend Cuthbert, who paraded up and down telling him, and anyone else who would listen, about his daring adventure in the wood.

High above, a distant cry echoed around the valley.
"Pee-ay! Pee-ay!"

Looking up, the birds could see two specks, circling and riding gracefully on the wind. It was a beautiful, peaceful afternoon and life was back to normal in Colin's garden. Wilberforce had learned his lesson.

Ozzie's Tale

Ozzie the cat was lonely. Ever since the old grey van had driven the family away from the house, he had roamed the streets looking for someone who cared enough to give him a new home. A few people fed him scraps, but that was all. At the end of each day he huddled into the corner by the door of the empty house, alone and sad.

That night he felt lonelier than ever. Around him, lights twinkled in windows and people laughed and chattered as they hurried home, eager to shut the door on the cold weather. Ozzie sighed and tried to tuck his paws even tighter underneath his tummy for warmth. He looked up at the starry sky and wondered why the stars seemed to sparkle brighter than ever.

As he watched, one star seemed to wobble and tumble across the sky. Ozzie blinked. Had it gone?

"Ouch!" said a voice, close by.

Ozzie sprang up, his fur bristling with fear.
"Who's that?" he hissed.

"Sorry!" purred the voice. "I slipped."

Ozzie peered 'round the corner and there, perched on the garden wall, was another cat. But not just any cat. This cat, although black and white like Ozzie, seemed to glow, from the tips of his ears to the end of his short, stumpy tail. Every time he moved, his fur sparkled as if coated with stardust. His eyes, as green as emeralds, gazed unblinkingly at Ozzie.

"Who are you?" whispered Ozzie, nervously.

The cat seemed to smile. "Well, I was once called Pippin Half-tail," he said thoughtfully. "I suppose I still am."

Ozzie was puzzled. But before he could ask anything else, Pippin stood up, stretched, then slowly sat down again wrapping his rather short tail round his paws.

"I was watching you," he remarked. "That's why I fell off my star."

"Me?!" gasped Ozzie. "Why?"

Pippin began to carefully lick a paw and wash behind his ears. Stardust drifted down towards Ozzie.

"Because," he answered at last, "I was lonely once. So, I'm going to help you."

"Are you really?" asked Ozzie, eagerly. Then he thought. "I don't have to fly, do I?"

Pippin stood up and stretched again. "Of course not, silly," he said. "Now come on. We haven't got all night!" And he set off, carefully, along the garden wall. Ozzie hastily scrambled up to join him and trotted after his new friend.

"Where are we going?" he called.

"To find someone who cares," came the reply.

Ozzie hardly dared to believe this. But then everything seemed unreal tonight.

As he followed the shimmering shape, flicking its short, stumpy tail, Ozzie glanced left and right into the houses and gardens they passed. Families sat watching flickering televisions, lights glowed behind bedroom curtains as children were tucked up in their beds. Delicious smells wafted from kitchens as tasty meals were prepared and Ozzie's tummy rumbled to remind him that he was hungry too.

Over walls, along fences they went. Around bushes and trees, then…Pippin stopped. He turned and came back to Ozzie. Gently rubbing noses, he seemed to shimmer even more.

"We're here," he purred. "It's over to you now. Good luck, my friend!"

Ozzie felt a soft rush of wind and blinked away a shower of tiny stars from his eyes. Rubbing his face with his paw, he peered through the trees into the garden of the nearest house.

At first, all he could see in the dark was an ordinary garden, shapes of plants and bushes and a twisting garden path, a garden seat, a shed, ornaments… Then, as the stars cleared from his eyes, he realised that the ornaments were actually cats! Perched on walls, among the bushes, along the path, cats of all shapes and sizes turned their eyes towards Ozzie.

He took a nervous step backwards as a large ginger and white cat came bustling up to him.

"Hello, I'm Bobby!" he cried. "Come and play!"

And before he knew what was happening, Ozzie was being led down the path, Bobby bouncing bossily beside him, introducing the cats who loomed out of the darkness.

"That's Daisy…been here ages! She's the boss, really."
"Yum-Yum…loves his food, that one."
"Candy…Yum-Yum's sister – not quite as big."
"Sooty…can you see her? It's easy to miss her when it's dark."
"Pru…yes, she is a big cat. It's all that fur!"
"Little Chap…careful! Not too good on his legs, that one."

A small black and white cat, with a slightly wobbly walk, nosed up to Ozzie and purred a welcome.

Then a beautiful cat with smoky grey fur and yellow eyes loomed over him.

"Bluebell," he announced. "Don't ask. I didn't pick it! Now let's hear about you."

And placing a large paw on Ozzie's nose, he gave a gentle push and Ozzie sat down with a bump.

Slowly, the cats circled him and listened as Ozzie explained where he came from and why he was alone. He didn't mention Pippin, because he was sure they would never believe him. When he had finished, he waited nervously, as dozens of eyes seemed to watch him intently. Then suddenly, the eyes seemed to vanish as all heads turned at the sound of a door opening. Light flooded into the garden and a voice called, "Supper!"
A bell tinkled and the cats, led by Bobby and Yum-Yum, headed for the door. Ozzie felt a gentle push in the back.

"Come on," whispered Daisy. "You're definitely one of us. They'll let you in."

Later, full of fish, Ozzie lay on a cushion, looking out on that magical garden, hardly daring to believe his luck. Around him, his new friends were curled up on chairs, or in beds and baskets. Shiny ornaments winked in the firelight and Ozzie could hear laughter from the television in the next room.

Daisy sat on the window ledge, staring out into
the moonlit garden.

"We're very lucky you know," she murmured. "All of us were lonely,
lost, unwanted. Then we found our way here.
No one gets sent away."

Ozzie purred contentedly.

"It doesn't matter," continued Daisy, "if you've got no teeth."
Ozzie yawned.

"A few fleas."
Ozzie scratched his ear.

"Or half a tail."
Ozzie sat bolt upright.

"Pippin!" he exclaimed. "Did he live here? Where is he?"

"Eh? What?" Daisy turned 'round and her eyes flashed
in the firelight.

"Pippin Half-tail," he explained.
"He found me and brought me here."

For a while, Daisy stared unblinkingly at Ozzie. Then, she slowly
turned, stretched and wrapping her tail round her paws, resumed
staring out at the night sky.

"He left a long time ago," came Bluebell's voice
from across the room.

"He won't come back," said Daisy.
"He always said he wanted to be a star."

Ozzie looked out of the window and up into the sky, to see one
very bright star winking down at them.

"Then his dream came true," he said and, with a satisfied purr,
he curled up into a ball.

Little Chap limped across to join him and snuggled next
to his new friend.

And with a contented purr, all the cats slept, while the star
shone brightly down.
Ozzie had, at last, found a home.

Norsworthy Needs a Wash

Norsworthy the gnome, had a large blob of bird poo on his head.
Well, let's be honest, if you stand under a tree for long enough
you can be sure all kinds of things will fall on your head.

Norsworthy had been draped in leaves, tickled by feathers, poked
by twigs and clouted by conkers.

He had also been snowed on, rained on, blown over and frozen.
He had been spattered in mud so often that he couldn't
remember what colour his trousers were.

And now, he had a large blob of bird poo on his head.

Norsworthy needed a wash.

A beady-eyed Robin sat on the fence looking down on the soil,
hoping to spot a tasty worm. His bright red breast glowed in
the sunshine.

"Morning, Norsworthy!" he chirruped. "Isn't it a lovely day?
Erm… What's that smell?"

At that moment, another robin flitted out of the tree.

"Oi! Hop it! This is my patch!"

There was a furious flurry of feathers as the two robins chased each other around the flowerbeds, over the pond and on to the branch above Norsworthy's head.

"Uh oh!" sighed Norsworthy.
Now he had two large blobs of bird poo on his head.

Norsworthy needed a wash.

A bee buzzed lazily among the early spring flowers. His black and gold stripes were dusted with pollen and his wings sparkled in the morning light.

Norsworthy sighed.

Mr Blackbird preened his glossy feathers and pecked daintily for grubs in the grass, with his bright yellow beak. He paused and cocked his head to one side, fixing his eyes on Norsworthy.

"Poo!" said Mr Blackbird.
Norsworthy glared.

With a loud chuckling call, Mr Blackbird flew to the highest branch of the tree. He ruffled his feathers and...

"Uh oh!" groaned Norsworthy.
Now he had three large blobs of bird poo on his head.

Norsworthy needed a wash.

Mr Blackbird sang his magical, musical song from his perch on the tree. Down in the pond the frogs croaked their own happy tune and a tiny wren darted in and out of the flowers near Norsworthy. Her perky little tail bobbed up and down as she hopped about. She paused and sniffed.

"Poo!"

"Thank you," said Norsworthy.

There was a rustle amongst the bushes. The little wren turned sharply and with a squeak of fright, flew up into the tree, just as the large black cat pounced!

"Phew!" gasped the wren.

"Uh oh…" moaned Norsworthy.
Now he had four large blobs of bird poo on his head.

Norsworthy needed a wash.

All was quiet in the garden now. Norsworthy dozed in the sun. A few petals of cherry blossom drifted from the tree and landed on the pond, like little boats.

A sudden beating of wings woke Norsworthy.

Blinking, he looked up.

In the tree was a pigeon...

No...two pigeons...

Hang on...

One, two, three, FOUR pigeons...

"Aaaargh!"

A door banged.

Maisie and her mum came down the path carrying a bucket of water and a scrubbing brush.

"Norsworthy has a lot of bird poo on him," remarked Maisie.

"Norsworthy needs a wash," said Mum, putting down her bucket and picking him up.

Splash!

Norsworthy was scrubbed and rubbed, until his blue jacket and red trousers gleamed.

Then they left him in the sun to dry.

Well away from the trees.

Now, Norsworthy has NO bird poo on his head.

He's had a very good wash indeed.

And the garden smells beautiful!

Elizabeth's Eyes

Elizabeth was cross.

She lay on her bed, gazing up at the roof and kicking her feet against the wall. The straw in the mattress prickled through her thin dress and she wriggled angrily to stop the itching. Then, with a squeal of temper, she swung herself round and on to the sandy floor with a thud. She glared sulkily around the empty room. Her mother was hard at work in the kitchens of the Big House and Elizabeth knew she should be helping by sweeping the floor of their own little home.

But today was her birthday! It just wasn't fair.

She stamped across to the door and flung it open. The lovely midsummer sun beamed in and she blinked in the bright light. Somewhere out there her father would be busy too, working in the gardens, helping to make everywhere splendid for the grand Midsummer Ball at the House that night.

Elizabeth would have loved to go to the Ball. She dreamed every day of wearing beautiful clothes and fine jewels like the ladies who would be there tonight. Her mother sometimes saw these marvelous things and would sit on her bed when she came home to tell her about it. Elizabeth imagined floating around the Great Hall in a dress of finest cream silk. It would show off her long, shining, golden hair, she knew. "Just like our Queen," her father would say proudly.

Instead, Elizabeth stood now and gazed at her patched and worn brown dress and stamped her foot. "She would never wear beautiful things," she thought miserably. And, even on her birthday, she couldn't think of anything to smile about.

Pushing her fists into her pockets, she stalked out into the gardens, kicking at stones and muttering under her breath as she went along. She was so busy feeling sorry for herself that she had wandered quite a long way through the gardens before she looked up. She found that she had left the main path and was in a part of the woodland which she did not know. She stopped and was about to turn 'round and go back, when she heard a noise.

Elizabeth frowned. It sounded like someone crying. Now, Elizabeth was really a kind little girl and she didn't like to think someone may be hurt, so she decided to explore. Slowly, she followed the path through the trees, pausing occasionally to listen for the sound. It gradually got louder and Elizabeth made her way towards it.

Eventually, she turned a corner and came upon a pond hidden in the trees. Water lilies floated on the dark surface and the sun, glinting through the leaves, made strange patterns on the water too.

Now, the sobbing noise was really close by. She looked more carefully at the edge of the pond and was amazed to see a tiny figure hunched on a stone at the water's edge. In fact, it was so tiny, she thought at first it was a frog! Peering closer, she saw a little man, dressed entirely in green, hunched up with his head on his arms. His tiny bell-shaped hat quivered miserably as he sniffed and whimpered to himself, and a pair of miniature wings drooped sadly over his shoulders.

Elizabeth didn't know what to do. She had heard of fairies, but had never seen one before. And she would never have imagined a fairy like this!

She was just wondering whether to say something – she didn't want to frighten him – when the little man spoke.
"So, you've come have you? I hope you're sorry!"

Elizabeth was so surprised that she sat down on the grass with a bump.

"Are you talking to me?" she whispered.

"Of course I am!" he snapped and Elizabeth found herself looking into an angry little face as the tiny green hat bobbed up. There was just one thing wrong. The tiny fairy's eyes stayed firmly shut. "Why are you so angry with me?" asked a puzzled Elizabeth. "I don't even know you!"

The fairy scrambled to his feet and Elizabeth hastily put out a hand as he wobbled dangerously on the rock.

"That's because you never look and listen!" he squeaked, his wings shimmering in the sun, as he stamped his tiny feet with rage. "Anyone born on Midsummer's Day can see fairies! They are the only people with this magic power. But YOU don't see anything!"

"I don't know what you mean!" cried Elizabeth, who was getting cross too. "And why don't you open your eyes and look at me?"

The fairy suddenly sat down again and sighed. "Because I can't," he said sadly.

"What do you mean?" asked Elizabeth, horrified.

"I am your very own fairy," explained the little man. "When you were born I was the fairy chosen to guard you. I've done my best, but I've failed." And he began to cry again.

Elizabeth wriggled closer and put out an anxious finger to touch the fairy. He sniffed and turned his back on her.

"I can't see because you can't see," he explained. "All you think about is yourself and what you want. You never look around and see the things which are really beautiful, so I can't see them either. When you learn to use your eyes, I will be able to use mine again too."

Elizabeth scrambled to her feet.
"I think you're silly," she grumbled, "I can see perfectly."

The little fairy shook his head so hard that he nearly
fell off the rock again.
"No! No!" he exclaimed.
"Wait! Listen to me! We only have until midnight!"

Elizabeth looked at his tightly closed eyes and hesitated.

"Have you ever seen a string of gleaming pearls?" asked the fairy.
"No," replied Elizabeth.

"A diamond on a bed of gold?"
"No."

"Clouds of lace on green silk?"
"No, never."

"Diamonds on black velvet?"
"No!" cried Elizabeth, shaking her golden hair furiously
and stamping her foot.

"Then you have until midnight to find them," cried the fairy. "If you
use your eyes, you will – and I will be able to use mine again too.
Now go!"

And before Elizabeth could speak, he had fluttered his wings and
vanished into a shaft of sunlight.

Elizabeth stood, open-mouthed, staring around her. The trees rustled in the breeze and the surface of the water rippled gently, causing the sunlight to break into a thousand sparkling pieces, but nothing else moved.

Slowly, Elizabeth began to walk back through the trees. Her little fairy's words danced around in her head as she puzzled over what he meant. As she walked, she idly brushed her hands against the grass and leaves beside the path. Suddenly, she felt the stickiness of a spider's web and pulled her hand back with an exclamation of annoyance. As she did so, she glanced down and saw the web quivering in the sunshine. Tiny droplets of morning dew still clung to the threads and they seemed to gleam, just like a string of pearls.

Elizabeth froze, staring at the web with delight. Was that it? Was this what he wanted her to see? She'd never noticed it before, it was true. She never looked at the lovely world around her, never saw the tiny things which made her world beautiful!

Running now, Elizabeth was soon out of the woods and into the garden. The gardeners glanced up in surprise, as they had seen the sulky little girl go into the woods earlier and here was someone quite different, her eyes sparkling with excitement. Elizabeth spotted her father among them and ran across the grass towards him.

"Now, then!" he exclaimed.
"What can have made my birthday girl so excited?"

"Father!" cried Elizabeth, tugging his sleeve. "Where can I find golden flowers? Or white lacy ones? Quickly!"

"Just one moment!" laughed her father. "Let me think!" Elizabeth danced impatiently at his side as he sat on the wall to think.

"The best golden flowers are not in these fancy gardens," he declared, after some thought. "You want the golden buttercups which cover the meadows. And look in the hedgerows for your lace."

"Thank you," beamed Elizabeth, and before he could say more, she planted a kiss on his cheek and scampered away. Sure enough, the meadows around the house glistened with golden buttercups and in the heart of each, sparkled a droplet of dew, just like a diamond.

In the hedgerows, the tall, white frothy flowers tossed their lacy heads against the glossy, green leaves of the bushes around them. Elizabeth was enchanted. She had never been so happy as she explored the countryside with new eyes, searching for the things her fairy had described. She found more golden flowers down by the stream and sat down to admire them, with her toes dipped in the ice-cold water. The fluffy clouds which skimmed over the sapphire-blue sky and the birds which swooped and glided gracefully against it, entranced her more than all the beautiful ladies she had ever dreamed of.

Only one thing troubled her now. Where were the diamonds on black velvet? Nothing in this magical world was black; whatever could he mean?

Finally, tired but happy, Elizabeth made her way home. Her feet were bare, her dress dusty, but her golden hair was garlanded with flowers and she floated towards the house like a princess. "Well?" said her mother, looking up from the pot of meat and herbs which she stirred over the fire. "I think you must have had a lovely birthday."

"Oh, I have!" sighed Elizabeth.
"But, Mama, there is one thing I can't find."

"And what is that?" asked her mother.

"I know it will sound silly," began Elizabeth.

Her mother smiled. "You are a Midsummer child," she said, "I think I will understand."

"Diamonds on black velvet," whispered Elizabeth. "I must find them! I can't let him down."

Elizabeth's mother didn't ask who she was talking about. In fact, like all mothers, she probably knew. Instead, after a quick glance towards Elizabeth's father, who sat quietly near the door enjoying the last of the sunshine, she took her daughter's hand and sat on the bench beside her.

"As a birthday treat," she smiled, "I think you may stay up a bit later. Then, you may find your answer."

Elizabeth was puzzled, but despite being tired, she didn't get cross. She helped to serve the meal and tidy the bowls, before sitting by the door with her father. Instead of listening enviously to the music and laughter drifting across from the big house, she watched the sun dip down in the sky, spreading a golden glow over the world. Bats skimmed around the trees and rooftops and the night-time scents from the flowers were better than any lady's perfume.

Gradually, night crept closer and stars began to prick little holes in the dark cloth of the sky. Elizabeth watched, as darkness fell and the stars shone brighter and brighter.

"Why don't you have a little walk?" suggested her father. "It will be safe tonight, I am sure."

Elizabeth had her answer now and was already scampering down the path. The stars were her diamonds, in their velvet sky! She ran into the gardens, and then stopped. In the darkness, it was hard to find the path into the woods and for a minute she thought she would never find it.

Then, as she listened, the most beautiful music came faintly to her ears. It could have been birds singing, water tinkling over stones, the wind in the trees, but Elizabeth knew it was fairy music.

Following the sound, she made her way into the trees and finally stood beside the hidden pool.

In front of her was an amazing sight. Fairies, glowing gold, silver and green, flitted overhead and danced in and out of the reeds. On the lake drifted a giant lily pad. On it sat the King and Queen of the fairies, garlanded with tiny flowers and wearing delicate silvery robes, sitting under a shimmering web of light spun by tiny spiders. They laughed as they sipped from miniature cups of golden nectar, watching glorious dragonflies dip and whirr over the water in a magical dance. And, as Elizabeth watched, she saw a tiny fairy at the Queen's feet, clapping his hands and beaming from ear to ear. She held her breath as he turned towards her, then all she could see were his two sparkling eyes; it was her very own fairy and he could see!

Spellbound, she watched as he flitted up to the Queen's side and whispered in her ear. The Queen nodded and Elizabeth saw the fairy take something from her, then he glided across the water to land on Elizabeth's arm.

"A gift from our Queen," he smiled and pressed something into her hand. "Thank you, my lady!" And, with a quaint little bow, he was gone.

Elizabeth knew it was time to go. She curtsied gracefully towards the fairies, then turned and hurried back down the path.
In the moonlight, she paused and opened her tightly closed fist. There, in her hand, was a tiny chain of the finest fairy silver. It gleamed and glistened like the stars overhead and Elizabeth found it just fitted around her wrist.

If any of the grand lords and ladies in the Big House that night had cared to look outside, they would have stopped and stared.

A little girl with golden hair, garlanded with flowers and wearing a dress which shimmered with the magic of fairy silver, was dancing over the grass as she made her way home.

A very happy little girl indeed.

Acknowledgements

Many thanks to Carole Chevalier for the beautiful illustrations which have brought my stories to life.

Also, thanks to Jude Lennon for encouraging me to get my work into print at last!

Also to my editor Sue Miller for her excellent advice and guidance and to Phil Burrows for being my technological guide and mentor.

To Sona and the wonderful Holloway cats, who inspired me to write 'Ozzie's Tale'.

Love and huge thanks as always, to Brian, Jane and Claire for their continued support and encouragement.

About the Author

Hello, from the Woodpecker Tree!

After thirty years in the teaching profession and now retired,
I have finally fulfilled my ambition to be a children's writer.

I grew up in Runcorn, before heading off to Yorkshire to study
teacher training at Ripon College of Education, then gaining my
English degree through Leeds University.

Since then, I have taught both at Secondary and Primary level, but it has
been the last 25 years working as a Primary teacher that has given me
much of the inspiration for my writing. There are few things better than
storytelling with young children, encouraging their own imagination to fly.

Tales from the Woodpecker Tree is a compilation of stories I have written
over the years and it is a joy to see them in print for the first time.

I'm hoping to follow this book with more stories from the Woodpecker tree,
including a collection of Christmas tales. Eventually, I hope to publish
a longer novel for older children and that project is well under way.

I hope you enjoy visiting the story seat among the branches of the
Woodpecker Tree and meeting the varied characters I found there!

To follow me and find out more about my children's stories, please visit::

www.lesleyrawlinsonauthor.co.uk

About the Illustrator

Bonjour! I'm Carole, a French graphic designer & illustrator. I grew up and studied graphic design in France and started my career as a creative in North Wales back in 2011. After more than 5 years living in this beautiful part of the world, I came back to France to continue pursuing my freelance career.

I started off specialising in illustration but quickly developed my skills and passion for all areas of graphic design. Even though I enjoy working on many fun projects, my true love is for colourful children's book illustration and beautifully hand-crafted typography.

I'm always very excited to work on fun and unique illustrations for books and I love bringing stories to life, using a lot of imagination and a touch of magic.

I've been honoured to create the whimsical illustrations for 'Tales from the Woodpecker Tree' and I truly hope that you'll enjoy reading it over and over!

www.carolechevalier.co.uk

50408316R00038

Made in the USA
Middletown, DE
30 October 2017